Miniphant to the Rescue

Cally Gee

CWR

PRINTED MARCH 2019

Editing, design and production by CWR.
Cover image: Cally Gee and CWR
Printed in the UK by Linney
ISBN: 978-1-78259-941-8

This book is dedicated to Belle, Josie, Reuben, Maki, Louis, Micah and Theo. You are already championing change every day.

I believe you can become life changers and world changers in time to come. I'm cheering you on – you can do it!

I would like to acknowledge Carolyn, Fi, Debz, Frances, Anna, Tracy and Debs. Your faith inspires me and many others to keep championing what we can change, keep trusting and living with what we can't yet change, and keep encouraging those around us to believe that they can live changed lives too.

Thank you to the one who can change all things but never changes Himself! His consistency, stability, faithfulness and grace are my rock. In God I put my trust.

Dear Mini Friend,

Hello! Welcome to another **Miniphant & Me** book.
My friends and I are so excited to share our adventures with you!
Our stories talk about:

thoughts in our head...

feelings in our heart...

and actions with our body...

because the way we think changes the way we feel and what we choose to do.
See if you can spot these in the story!

Every day, we do lots of different things at different times. Our lives are full of changes – most small, some big, many planned and a few unexpected or out of our control.

Do you ever feel like Cat? She doesn't like things to change or be different – she likes things to remain how they are. But change can be good, as we will find out in this story.

We will also learn that 'change' changes things! It can change the way we think and feel. We can even discover key ways to becoming 'Champions of Change'.

There is so much to learn about change, but we hope this book is a starting point to help you along the way. At the back, you will find some Animal Friend Fact Files, Bedtime Thoughts and Daytime Fun activities. I'll tell you more about them at the end of the story.

Love, **Miniphant** x

One last thing: see if you can spot **all** the keys hidden in the story!

It was a windy day, and not just because of the weather – it was coming from Miniphant too!

'Oopsie-poopsie-pardon!' he trumped.

'I've eaten too many beans,' he thought to himself while enjoying his 'windy' walk.

Looking up, Miniphant saw Robin flying high up in the sky.

'What's going on up there?' Miniphant asked.

'I'm waiting for the wind to change!' Robin chirped back.

'Oh! Sorry, that's my fault!' Miniphant replied.

'Not your wind, Miniphant, the weather's wind! The key to wind power is knowing how best to use it to help me fly,' Robin explained, having had a lot of experience.

Miniphant liked the idea of 'wind power'. He watched and waited for Robin to join him.

Getting impatient, he asked, 'How long will we have to wait for the wind to change?'

'I don't know, Miniphant. We just have to wait patiently and trust that it will happen,' said Robin, flapping his wings. '**Patience** is something that we can learn and grow inside us as we wait. It is one of the keys to becoming a Champion of Change!' he twittered.

Miniphant liked the idea of being a 'champion' of something, but practising patience and finding keys sounded challenging.

'If we learn to accept that changes are a part of life, we'll be ready for them when they come our way,' Robin continued. 'Some we choose and plan for, while others happen unexpectedly!'

Just at that very moment, while Robin was busy talking, a **HUGE** gust of wind blew from the opposite direction, sending Robin W H O o O o O S H headfirst into the garden pond reeds!

'Wow!' trumped Miniphant. 'Are you OK, Robin?'

'As I was saying,' came a muffled voice, 'unexpected changes <u>and</u> accidents happen from time to time, but it's how we respond and what we learn from them that's important.' Robin popped out of the reeds holding his wing. 'When you have been flying as long as I have, you get used to the odd bumpy landing. It hurts but I'll recover, and I'll fly again. Now where's my first aid kit?'

As Miniphant gently bandaged Robin's wing, Robin said to him,

'Being able to carry on when unexpected things happen is called being resilient. It's another key to becoming a Champion of Change!'

Miniphant nodded, trying to say the big word in his head and remember all the 'keys' he needed, but not really believing he ever would.

Later that morning, Mole appeared, dressed in her swimming gear.

'Can you two teach me how to swim underwater?' she asked Miniphant and Robin. 'I spend my whole life living underground, so I thought it was time for a change!'

'We would love to!' Robin chirped. 'Miniphant can get in the water. He's an excellent swimmer!'

'Me! Teach?' Miniphant was doubtful whether he had the confidence.

'Yes! Your trunk is already like a snorkel, and your ears are like flippers,' said Robin.

'And your trumps are like a propeller helping you go faster!'

Mole giggled.

Miniphant was a little embarrassed, but also proud of his skills.

'OK, Mole, let's do it!' Miniphant tooted.

'You really are becoming a Champion of Change, Miniphant,' Robin said proudly. 'Having <u>confidence</u> that you can do things and <u>asking for help</u> are two more keys you need.'

Miniphant felt more confident but wished he knew where to find all these keys.

While Robin gave instructions, Miniphant showed Mole how to swim underwater. Bravely, Mole swam deeper into the water, becoming more and more confident.

'I can see something sparkling at the bottom of the pond. Why don't you swim down to find out what it is?'

called Robin.

Mole felt she had learnt enough to give it a go, so she and Miniphant swam down towards the shiny object.

As they got closer, they saw that it was a _real_ key. Mole picked it up, and they swam back to Robin as quickly as they could. After reaching the top and taking a deep breath, they shouted, 'It's a key. It's a key!'

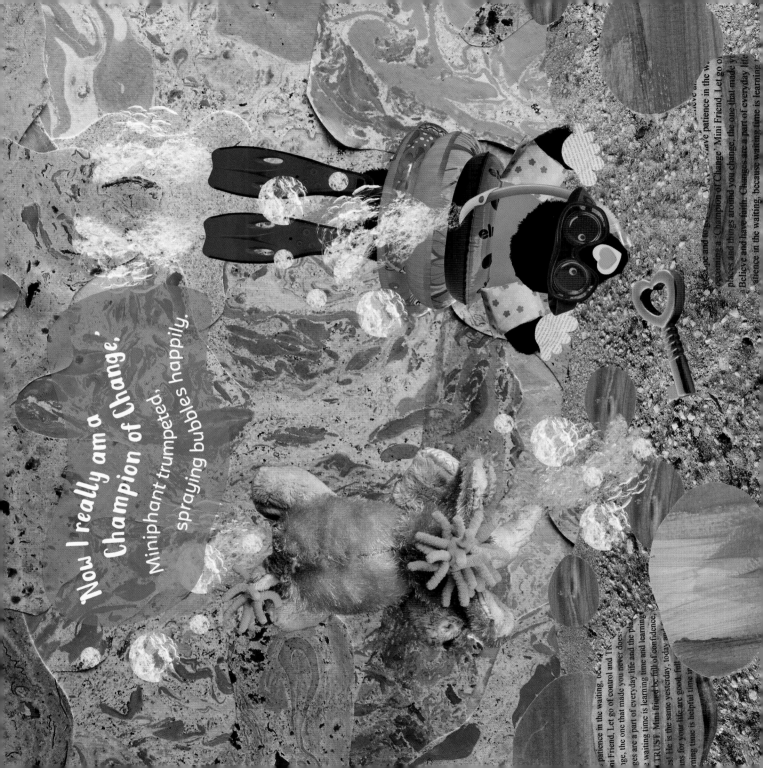

'Now I really am a
Champion of Change,'
Miniphant trumpeted,
spraying bubbles happily.

'Well done for getting the key,' said Robin, 'but the keys to being a Champion of Change aren't <u>real</u> keys. They are active thoughts like <u>patience</u>, <u>resilience</u>, having <u>confidence</u>, <u>trusting</u>, and <u>asking for help</u>,' he continued. 'You might not feel like much of a champion at the moment, but change your thinking to believe you can be, and keep trying!'

Miniphant smiled boldly as he wrote these 'keys' on his suitcase lid.

Cat had been watching her three friends from the other side of the pond. Not wanting to get wet, she had stayed away from the swimming lesson, but the wind howled around her and she couldn't hear what was being said.

She moved a bit closer. Suddenly, she slipped on the pond reeds. **Whoooosh** went the wind and **splaaaash** into the pond went Cat!

'Heeeellllpppp!'

she meowed loudly, splashing about in the water with her paws. Cat didn't know how to swim, so all she could do was **trust** that help <u>would</u> come – quickly!

Miniphant believed he could help, so he jumped into action.

'Come on, Mole and Robin, we must rescue Cat!'

He quickly turned his suitcase into a boat, and they set off across the pond.

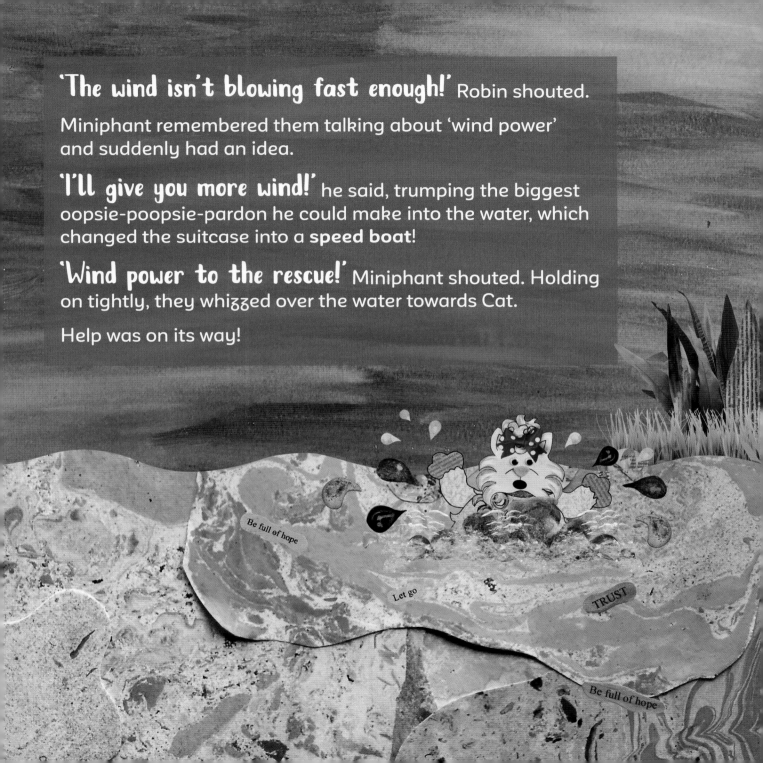

'The wind isn't blowing fast enough!' Robin shouted.

Miniphant remembered them talking about 'wind power' and suddenly had an idea.

'I'll give you more wind!' he said, trumping the biggest oopsie-poopsie-pardon he could make into the water, which changed the suitcase into a **speed boat!**

'Wind power to the rescue!' Miniphant shouted. Holding on tightly, they whizzed over the water towards Cat.

Help was on its way!

Be full of hope

Let go

TRUST

Be full of hope

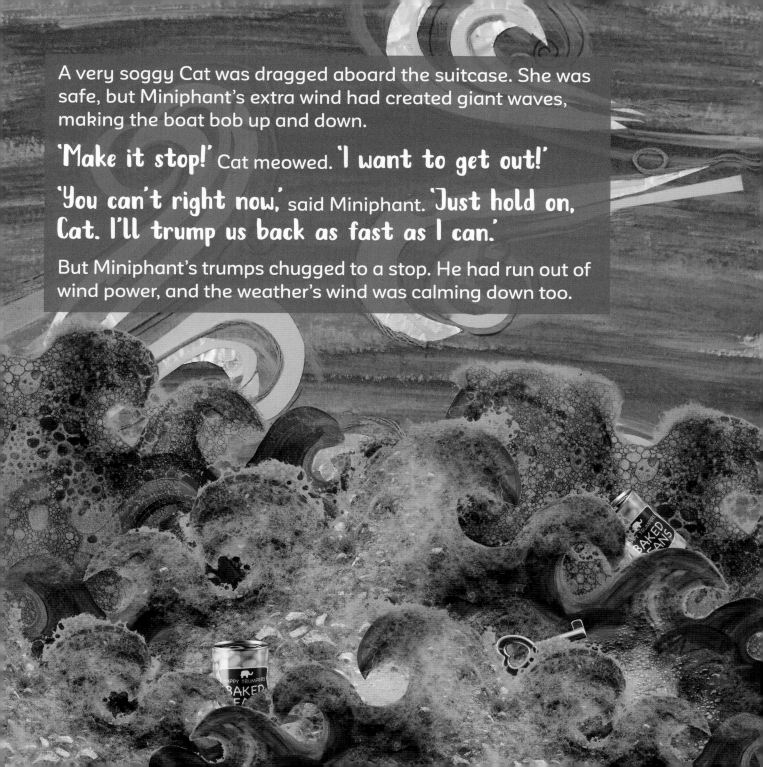

A very soggy Cat was dragged aboard the suitcase. She was safe, but Miniphant's extra wind had created giant waves, making the boat bob up and down.

'Make it stop!' Cat meowed. 'I want to get out!'

'You can't right now,' said Miniphant. 'Just hold on, Cat. I'll trump us back as fast as I can.'

But Miniphant's trumps chugged to a stop. He had run out of wind power, and the weather's wind was calming down too.

The four friends were stuck in the
middle of the pond on their boat.
Finding it hard to trust, Cat yowled,
'Now what's going to happen?'

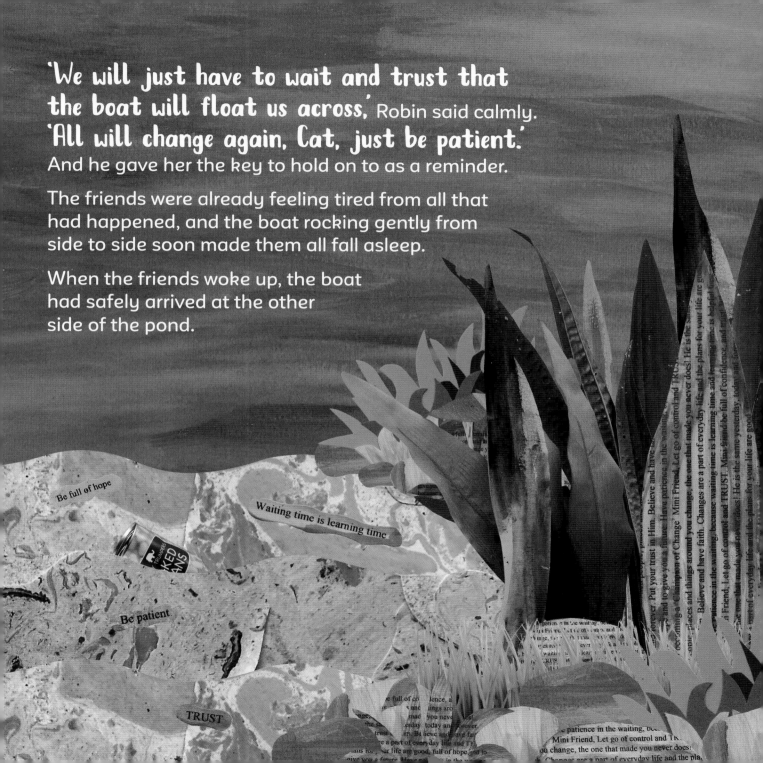

'We will just have to wait and trust that the boat will float us across,' Robin said calmly. 'All will change again, Cat, just be patient.' And he gave her the key to hold on to as a reminder.

The friends were already feeling tired from all that had happened, and the boat rocking gently from side to side soon made them all fall asleep.

When the friends woke up, the boat had safely arrived at the other side of the pond.

Be full of hope

Waiting time is learning time

Be patient

TRUST

Back on land, the friends huddled together. Feeling stronger than ever, they thought about what had happened. Each of them had been changed by the day's events. Each of them were thankful for getting through the challenges. And each of them had found the keys to becoming Champions of Change.

'We did it!' said Mole excitedly.

'I knew we'd get here if we believed,' said Robin.

'What a relief!' said Cat, still dripping wet.

Miniphant tooted happily as one of his tins of beans floated towards him.

'Oh, goodie!' he said. 'More _wind_ power!'

They all laughed.

You are a Champion of Change

Animal Friend Fact Files

Here are some other ways that the animals champion change in their everyday lives, which Mini Friends might find helpful.

Robin suggested that I have a go at teaching Mole how to swim underwater. At first, I didn't feel confident and was very nervous, but I tried to believe in the encouragement that Robin and Mole gave me. Very quickly, I found that I had skills to teach Mole.
Mini Friend, next time you have an opportunity to make a change and try something different like a new sport or activity, why not give it a go! You might find you really enjoy it!

Thank you, Miniphant, for teaching us how to be brilliant Champions of Change!

Familiar voices and pawing my lovely soft fluffy tail help me to feel reassured and comforted when changes are happening.
Mini Friend, I understand that living through changes isn't always easy. You might be reassured by hearing your grown-up's kind voice. Or perhaps you have a special soft toy or blanket that comforts you like my tail comforts me.

These are super ways to help us live as Champions of Change, Cat!

I find that I often learn something in times of waiting. It is also a good opportunity to practise being patient and trusting. A good tip to becoming confident about living with new or unexpected changes is to watch how others respond to changes, ask questions and listen to the answers. That's what Miniphant did when he watched me flying. Useful tips from others help you to feel more equipped and confident when changes happen around you.

Thanks for sharing what you've learnt about becoming a Champion of Change, Robin!

Sometimes my hills get stamped on by other animals or humans but I try not to let it upset me. Although they were good hills, I quickly start thinking about how a new one could be even better. I can't control what others do, but I **can** control how I respond. I enjoy building anyway so I try to respond resiliently and trust that things will get better.

Mini Friend, have you ever built a tower or painted a picture and it has got spoilt by someone else? Next time something like that happens, try to respond like I would, and trust that what has happened will be sorted out fairly.

Great example of being a Champion of Unexpected Change, Mole!

Bedtime Thoughts and Daytime Fun

Hello again, Mini Friend!

I hope you enjoyed the story and want to be a Champion of Change now too?

Did you spot all the hidden keys?

Here are some more things we can do together.

Bedtime Thoughts

Grown-ups: you can use these thinking, whispering and listening activities as part of the bedtime routine, enhancing your child's emotional literacy, mental health, and spiritual wellbeing. They are designed to be calming and settling, thought provoking, and comforting at the end of the day.

Emotional Literacy

We have lots of different feelings about the many changes that happen every day. Some changes, like surprises and adventures, might feel fun and exciting. However, other changes might make us feel differently. When that happens, try practising some of the 'active thinking' keys from the story: **Patience**, **Resilience**, **Confidence**, **Asking for Help**, and **Trusting**. When we do that, we can begin to become Champions of Change and start to think and feel more hopeful.

You can't always stop changes happening but you can change how you think about them. Remember, feelings come to visit but they don't have to stay. Choose to think like a champion and your heart will start feeling like one too.

To think about

The keys hidden in the book have a little heart on them. Sometimes, the way we think about changes makes a difference to how we feel about them in our hearts. Think of your heart as a door to visiting feelings. Now pretend you have your own little heart key that can open or shut your heart door to different feelings.

The keys in the story help us to grow in our hearts and minds. The more we practise those keys, the easier it will become to look after our hearts by deciding which feelings we can hold on to, and which feelings we can let go.

Mental Health

Some changes, like growing, we do without thinking – but there are other changes that might need some planning and thought before we do them. For example, a grown-up might tell you to start finishing what you are doing because you will soon be doing something else. It can be hard to follow their instructions when you are doing something enjoyable or don't want to do a new activity. At those times, you have a choice. You can either ignore or forget what your grown-up has said, or you can accept what you are being asked to do as a way of showing that you trust the grown-up. Learning to live with little changes can help you to prepare for bigger ones. When you believe and trust your grown-up then, together with them, you can champion any changes.

When bigger changes happen, we might need a bit more time to get ready for them. The more prepared we are, hopefully the less we will worry about big changes. Maybe a new baby is coming soon to join your family. Perhaps you are moving house, starting school, or saying goodbye to someone you might not see for a while. All these changes need time to prepare for, so that minds, hearts and bodies can be ready for when the change comes. Waiting time can be learning time – helping us to get ready!

Ask your grown-up to print off the certificate on Miniphant's website that says that you are a Champion of Change. Place it somewhere where you can see it to remind you that you can keep being a champion every day, no matter what changes come your way!

Spiritual Wellbeing

Jesus is Miniphant's friend and He wants us to know that, even though our lives will be full of change, He **never** changes! He is always there, always loving and always ready to help. You can rely on Him for anything and everything. The Bible says that Jesus is the same yesterday and today and forever. All we have to do is believe and trust Him. This isn't easy when things are out of our control but He wants to teach us and help us.

There is a story in the Bible about Jesus being asleep on a boat during a storm. Everyone in the boat was feeling worried, scared, confused and tired by the journey. They couldn't believe that Jesus was fast asleep and said to Him, 'How can you sleep at a time like this? Do something!'

The people in the boat could not control the storm, but instead of trusting Jesus, they worried. Jesus was able to sleep because He trusted in God, His heavenly Father, who He believed **was** in control. This was why He was able to sleep in peace. However, He also wanted His friends in the boat to be at peace, so He told the waves to stop and the storm to calm.

We can always trust that Jesus will be with us and what He says is true especially when we, or people close to us, are going through changes.

To think about

As you go to sleep tonight, imagine your bed is a boat. Think about all the changes you are living with right now and whisper them to God. Ask Him to calm the 'storm' in your head, so you can sleep peacefully and dream of adventures as a Champion of Change with the BEST champion of all – Jesus! Jesus loves you so much and wants to help you with every change that comes your way.

Daytime Fun

Grown-ups: these activities are designed to be interactive, fun and creative and can be integrated into your child's day to enhance their social awareness, physical wellbeing and creative thinking.

Physical Activity: Change it, Dance it

Listening to music and dancing often changes the way you are feeling. Dancing also helps you to express yourself by moving your body as you listen to music. Why not make up your own dance to show the changes you might be going through? How are you feeling? What movements could you make to show those feelings? Dancing your feelings might help you to live through the changes better.

You could also make up a dance to show a change taking place in something, like a caterpillar turning into a butterfly or a tadpole becoming a frog.

Choose a change to create a dance to. Then ask your grown-up to find some music that doesn't have any words, and make up a dance to show the changes happening. If you are going to dance a tadpole becoming a frog, you could start curled up into a ball and slowly unfold into a swimming tadpole moving around the floor. You could then pretend to grow some legs and start to jump. Finally, you could grow some arms and begin to leap like a frog. Listen to the music to help you move in time with the beat or the rhythm of the tune. This helps you know when to change your position. Try to notice how it feels to move and change your body shape as the music gets louder and quicker or becomes softer and slower.

After you have practised a few times, why not put on a dance show in your living room? Or just enjoy the freedom of movement for yourself. Hopefully, it will help you relax and express the changes you are feeling, and even change the way you end up feeling about them.

Social Activity: Seasonal Walk – Let Your Senses Talk

Walking is great exercise and you can do it all year round with friends or family. Next time you go for a walk, collect some of nature's treasures (like pinecones and leaves) along the way. Use your senses of sight, hearing, smell and touch to answer the following questions:

• What was the best thing you saw on the walk? Why was it your favourite part?
• Was there anything you smelt on the walk? What was it and how would you describe the smell?
• What did you touch and feel on your walk? Where did you find it?
• What sounds did you hear on your walk? Can you try and make the same sound?

When you return home from your walk, you could talk about, draw and write down the answers to the above questions. You might even like to make a collage using the natural treasures you found.

If you go on the same walk again at a different time of year, look at how the trees, bushes and flowers have changed from one season to the next. Use the questions to help you think and talk about the changes around you. Can you spot the differences from the last time you went?

Creative Activity: Pond Painting Play

Ask your grown-up if you can do some painting and make a pond. Get a small square canvas frame and turn it upside down (if you don't have a canvas frame, use a small low-sided box). Paint the inside of the frame watery colours like blue, green and grey. Paint the sides of the frame green. Make some flowers, reeds, grasses out of paper to decorate the edges. You could also find some small stones to put inside. Find an even smaller box (maybe an empty match box), paint and decorate it to look like Miniphant's suitcase.

Go to Miniphant's webpage for extra help if needed.

Using other small toy animals, you could imagine the characters and make up your own rescue adventures and swimming games. As your story moves forward, your characters could grow in confidence and resilience.

Creative Activity: Keys to Being a Champion

To remind you of the keys to living as Champions of Change, draw your own set of keys or print off the key templates on Miniphant's webpage, colour them in and cut them out. You could decorate them with sparkly paper, foil and shiny stickers too. Make sure you have one for each of the keys you need to practise. Tie some string through them all and hang them by your bed or, even better, by a mirror. Every morning, look at the keys and then into the mirror, and tell yourself you can try and be a Champion of Change every day!

For all templates, certificates and additional help, head over to Miniphant's webpage at **cwr.org.uk/miniphant**

It's time to say goodbye, Mini Friend. I'm believing in you! Go and be a **Champion of Change**. I hope you come and join me and my friends for more adventures in our other books.

See you **oopsie-poopsie** soon!

Love,

Miniphant x

Join Miniphant and friends for more adventures!

Miniphant Moves In

Explores: Identity and self-worth

One Big Adventure

Explores: Courage

The Magnificent Raspberry Mountain

Explores: Managing anger

Seeds, Weeds and Spaghetti Trees

Explores: Feelings of Jealousy

For more information about the **Miniphant & Me** series,
including additional Daytime Fun activities, thoughts from the Bible and lots more, visit

cwr.org.uk/miniphant